W9-BLO-428
WILLOUGHBY
& THE LION

THE BOWEN PRESS
An Imprint of HarperCollins*Publishers*

Willoughby & the Lion

Manufactured in China.

www.harpercollinschildrens.com

Illustration on pages 26–27 inspired by
crowd photograph copyright © 2007 Michael Halsband

Library of Congress Cataloging-in-Publication Data
Foley, Greg.
Willoughby & the lion / by Greg Foley. — 1st ed.
p. cm.
Summary: When Willoughby moves to a new house far away from his friends, he meets an enchanted lion who shows him what is truly important in life.
ISBN 978-0-06-154750-8 (trade bdg.) — ISBN 978-0-06-154751-5 (lib. bdg.)
[1. Friendship—Fiction. 2. Wishes—Fiction. 3. Magic—Fiction. 4. Lions—Fiction.]
I. Title. II. Title: Willoughby and the lion.
PZ7.F35Wi 2008 2008000430 [E]—dc22 CIP AC

Set in Futura Medium

09 10 11 12 13 LEO 10 9 8 7 6 5 4 3 2
❖
First Edition

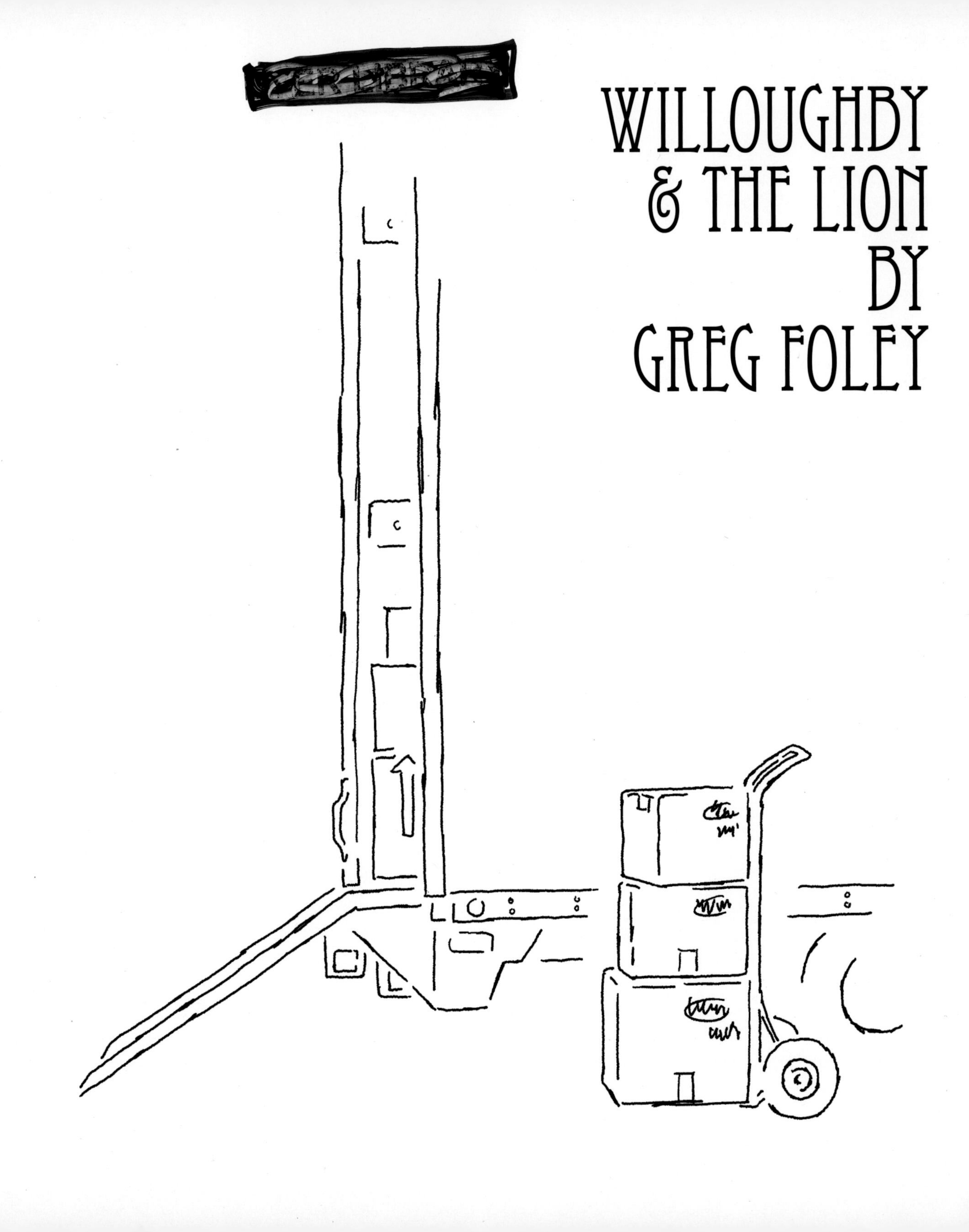

WILLOUGHBY & THE LION

BY GREG FOLEY

For you.

Willoughby Smith hated his new house. It was much smaller than his old house and too far away from any kind of a friend.

There were no trees. And right in the middle of the back yard was a big rock.

One morning, Willoughby saw something strange through his window. Sitting on top of the rock was a magnificent golden lion.

"Excuse me," Willoughby said. "What are you doing in my back yard?"

The lion turned to Willoughby. "I've got the power to grant you ten wishes," he said. "But unless you wish for the most wonderful thing of all, I'll be stuck on this rock forever."

Willoughby thought for a moment. "It would be wonderful if this were a bigger house," he said.

The lion closed his eyes, and Willoughby wondered what he was up to. Suddenly, the lion asked, "Is that big enough?"

There stood a palace where the house used to be. It was more wonderful than Willoughby could have imagined. And he ran inside, where his parents were celebrating.

The next day, Willoughby came to the lion and said, "I wish I had a roller coaster to ride."

The lion closed his eyes. Soon, high and winding tracks rose up all around the yard.

Willoughby jumped into the middle car and headed toward the top. He called down to the lion, "Hey, Lion! I wish I weren't alone up here."

In an instant, he wasn't.

Every day, Willoughby went to the lion with another wish. For his fourth wish, Willoughby asked for the fastest shoes in the world.

For his fifth wish, he asked for shoes that were even faster.

His sixth wish was for a hot-air-balloon-submarine (with an escape helicopter).

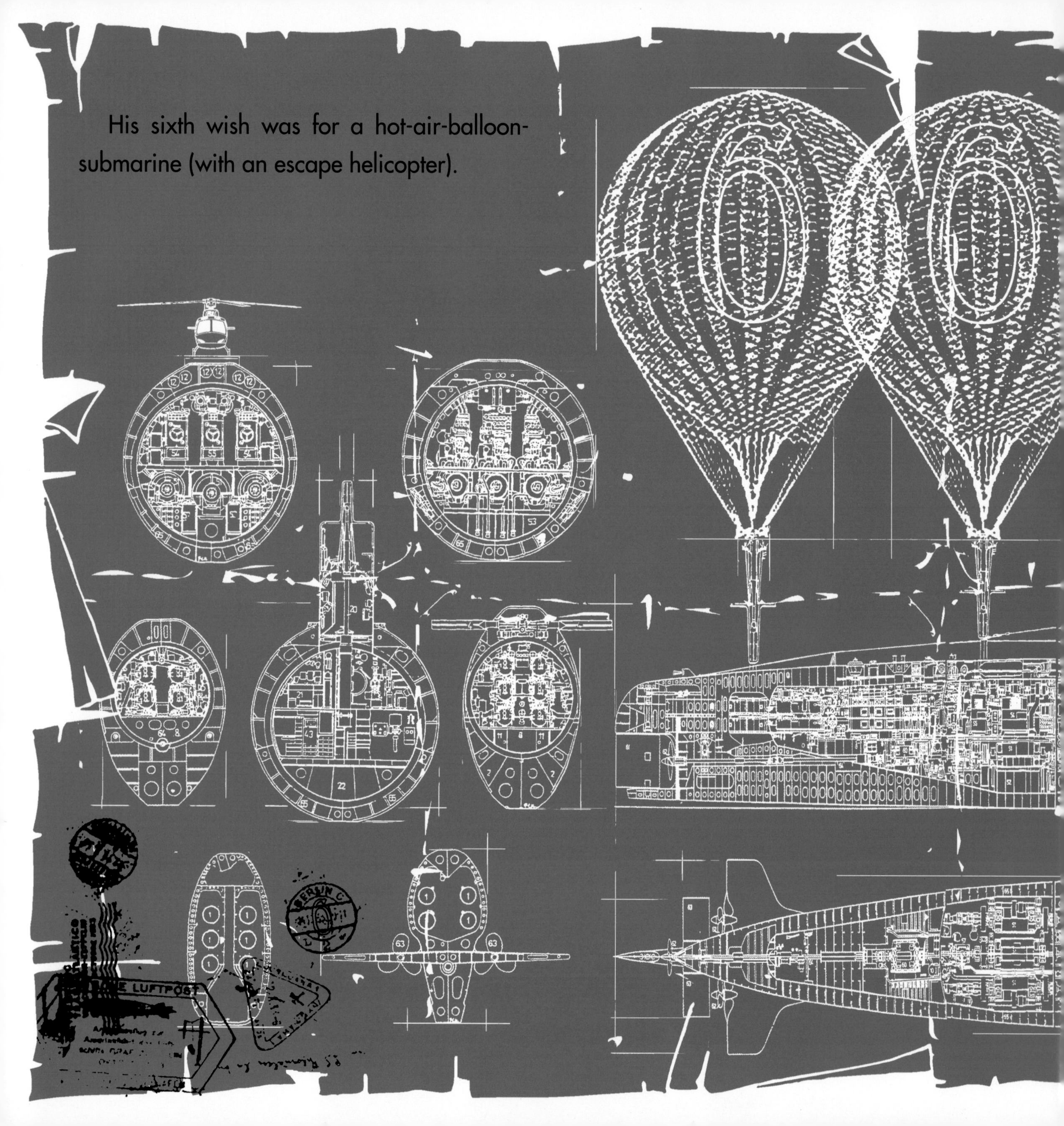

Graf Zeppelin
KRALJEVINA JUGOSLAVIJA
Semena
Montevideo.
Uruguay

After a while, Willoughby became hungry. "How about something to eat, Lion?" he said.

Out of thin air appeared the seven tallest cakes in the world, each piled high with cookies and candy.

Next, Willoughby wished for a pair of X-ray glasses. Then he was granted a set of ancient books with all the answers to any kind of homework.

By this time, there were crowds pushing and shoving to catch a glimpse of Willoughby and his enchanted lion.

But even after nine wishes, Willoughby hadn't wished for the most wonderful thing of all.

Under the shadow of the roller coaster, Willoughby found the lion slumped on the rock, with his head hung low.

"What's the matter?" Willoughby asked.

The lion looked up. "I miss my home," he said. "I want to run through the fields with all the other lions."

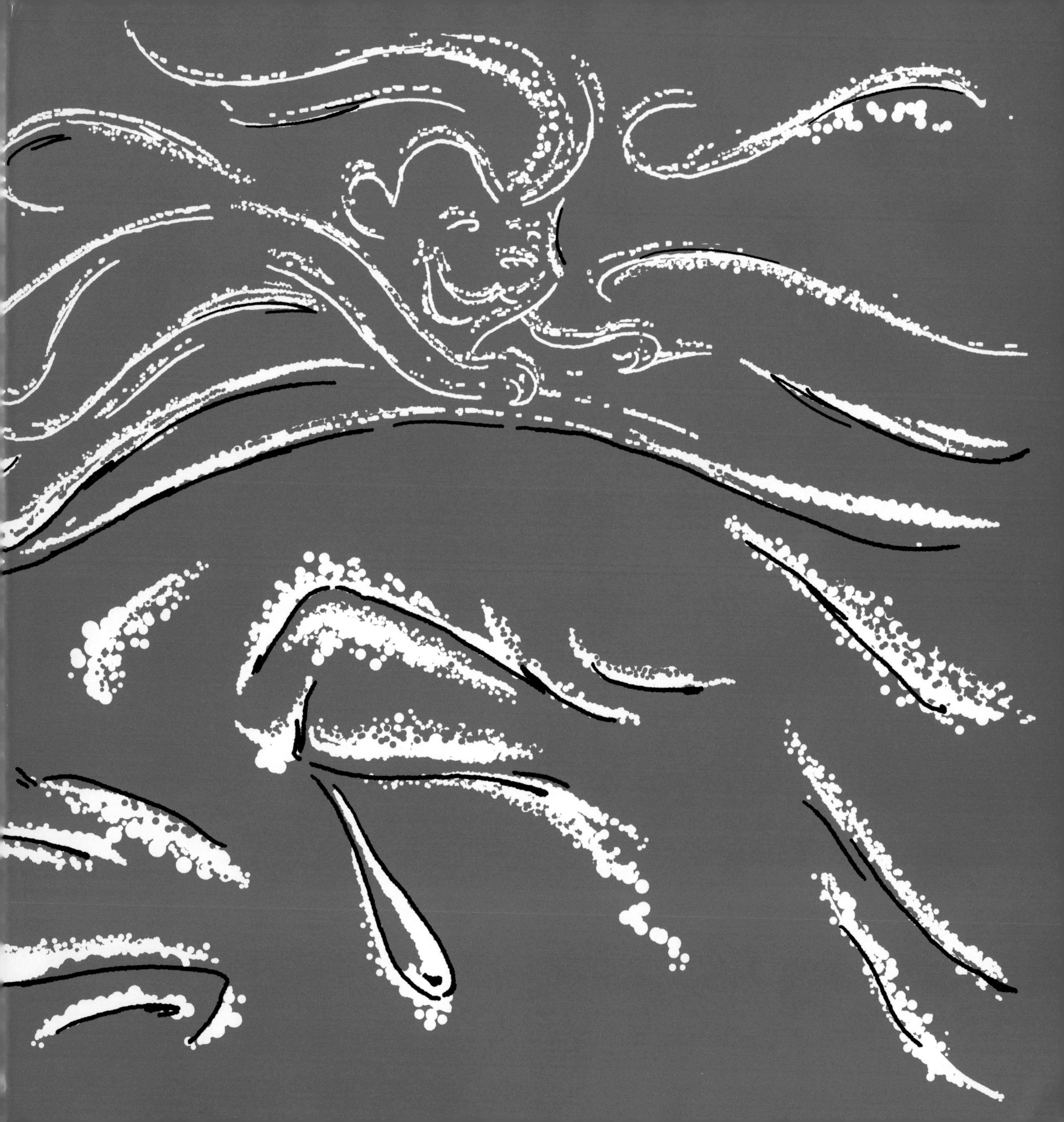

For the first time, Willoughby sat down next to the lion and tried to cheer him up. He told the lion everything he could remember about his old house. Then he told him the best jokes he knew.

Together, they sang loud songs and practiced roaring until they were out of breath.

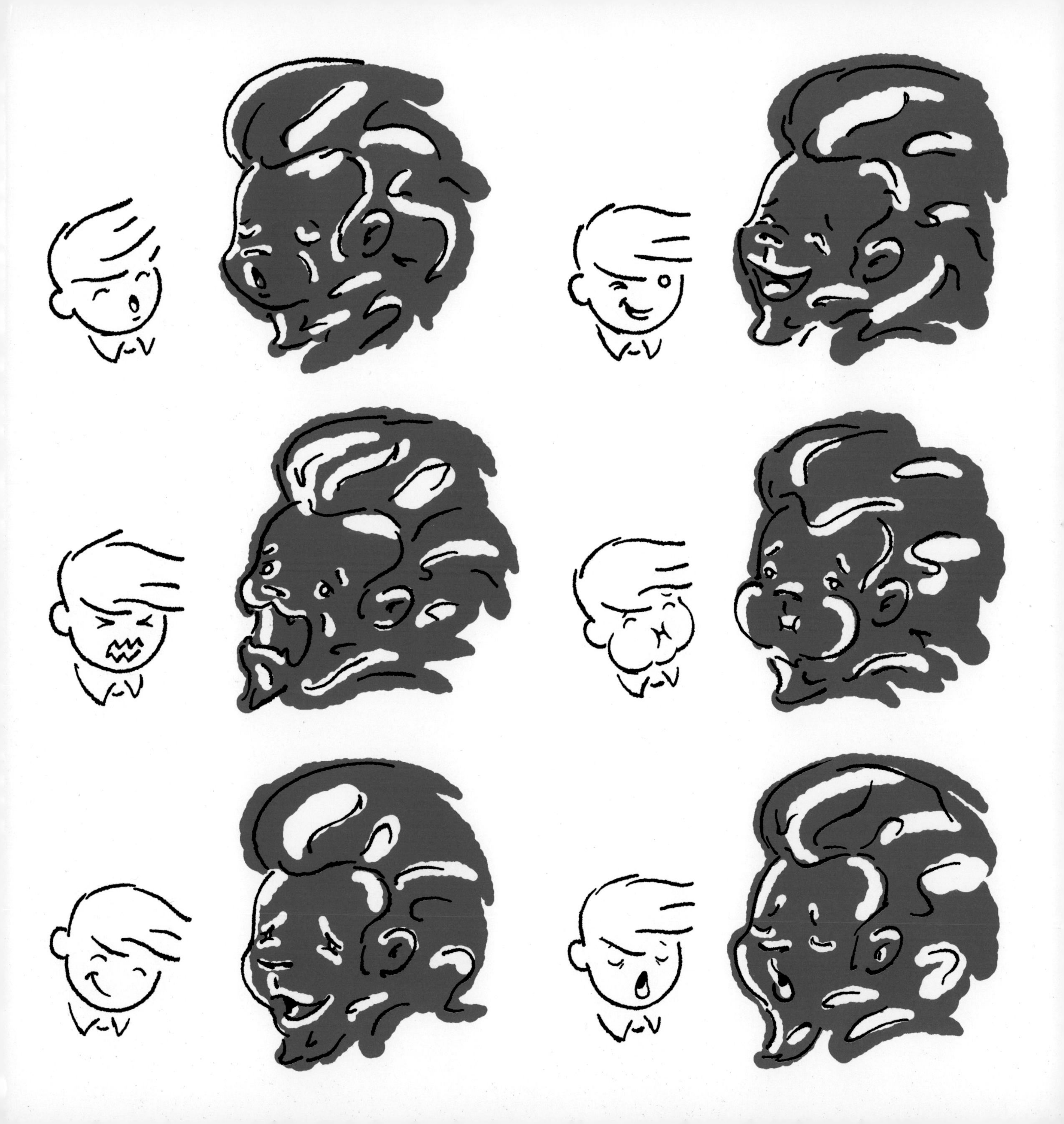

As it became dark, Willoughby looked around at all the things he'd wished for. Then he realized what would be even more wonderful.

He whispered his last wish into the lion's ear and drifted off to sleep at the foot of the big rock.

When Willoughby woke up, everything seemed different. A cozy house stood in the middle of an open yard. The roller coaster was gone, and so were the crowds of people.

Willoughby looked up at the big rock. But the lion was no longer there. In his place, there was a small gold coin with two words printed on it. Willoughby picked up the coin to have a closer look. . . .

It said: TRUE FRIEND.